To Sanda and Bogdan, with a big friendly hug!

First published in 2015 by Child's Play (International) Ltd
Ashworth Road, Bridgemead, Swindon SN5 7YD, UK

Published in USA by Child's Play Inc
250 Minot Avenue, Auburn, Maine 04210

Distributed in Australia by Child's Play Australia Pty Ltd
Unit 10/20 Narabang Way, Belrose, NSW 2085

ISBN 978-1-84643-732-8
CLP160115CPL03157328

Printed in Shenzhen, China

1 3 5 7 9 10 8 6 4 2

A catalogue record of this book
is available from the British Library

www.childs-play.com

CRUNCH!

Carolina Rabei

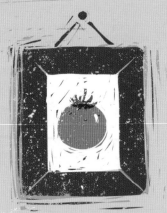

This is **Crunch.**

Crunch likes
his comfy bed,
but most of all
he loves...

Yum yum!

Brrrrrr!

Crunch
had everything
he needed to be happy.
But there was something
missing from his life...

...though he didn't know what.

No way!

My food is **MY** food!

...A hug.
A friendly hug.
How about a
big friendly hug?!

Crunch finished
his fresh breakfast.

But then he started
to think about Cheddar.

I wonder where Cheddar is now?

He looked so skinny and hungry.
I'm sure he could have eaten **ALL** my food.

I wonder if he has found any?
He might be **starving**...

...or in **real danger!**

Oh no!

I kept my food,
but I lost a friend!

Cheddar, I'm coming!

Anyone here?

Hey, have you seen a mouse?

Maybe here?

Oh, this smells tasty!

Cheddar! Where are you?

Oh, WOW!

I'm sorry, my friend!

Sorry for what?

For not giving you
a hug!